For my grandmother,
who always brought
apple pie
—H.M.Z.

Text copyright © 2005, 2009 by Harriet Ziefert
Illustrations copyright © 2005, 2009 by Amanda Haley
All rights reserved / CIP Data is available.
Published in the United States by
 Blue Apple Books
515 Valley Street, Maplewood, N.J. 07040
www.blueapplebooks.com
Distributed in the U.S. by Chronicle Books
Printed in China   4/10
ISBN: 978-1-593540-70-8
7 9 10 8

41 USES
for a
GRANDMA

Harriet Ziefert

drawings by Amanda Haley

 BLUE APPLE BOOKS

1.
security blanket

2.
partner

3.
thermometer

4.
lounge
chair

5. dance instructor

6.
page turner

7. hair braider

8.
personal
shopper

9. keeper
of secrets

10.
ballet barre

11. e-pal

12. play date

13.
bearer
of
gifts

14. someone to love you when others may not

15. timekeeper

16. movie companion

17. coatroom

18. Fan club

19.
mini kitchen

20.
jewelry box

21.
baby-sitter

22.
marathon runner

23. restaurant companion

24. pillow

25. valentine

26.
after-school
friend

27.
yoga
teacher

28. vacation destination

29. chef

30. towel rack

31. swim
instructor

32. builder

33. history teacher

34.
monkey bars

35.
welcome mat

36. lifeguard

37. hiding place

38. decorator

39. pet sitter

40.
ticket
holder

41. friend

THE END